# BLACKTOP
## FRANK

2/2018
JE

To Linds, Stephanie and Mr. Ryan, for

telling me I was good enough—LA

GROSSET & DUNLAP
Penguin Young Readers Group
An Imprint of Penguin Random House LLC

Text copyright © 2017 by Penguin Random House LLC. Cover illustration
copyright © 2017 by Raul Allen. All rights reserved. Published by
Grosset & Dunlap, an imprint of Penguin Random House LLC,
345 Hudson Street, New York, New York 10014. GROSSET & DUNLAP
is a trademark of Penguin Random House LLC. Printed in the USA.

*Library of Congress Cataloging-in-Publication Data is available.*

ISBN 9781101995662 (paperback)          10 9 8 7 6 5 4 3 2 1
ISBN 9780451533593 (library binding)     10 9 8 7 6 5 4 3 2 1

# BLACKTOP

## FRANK

## BY LJ ALONGE

Grosset & Dunlap
An Imprint of Penguin Random House

# CHAPTER 1
# PARADISE

I'm sprinting up the sideline when I catch an outlet pass from Janae. Homegirl likes to throw passes that make your palms sting, the kind that leave a mark. I stop at the top of the key to look around the court. Life Lesson #553: When you're vertically challenged, you've got to think your way to the rim. In front of me is a Foot Locker All-Star, a guy with a neon headband and neon arm-sleeve and a pair of shoes that would take me a whole summer of hustling to cop. He spits in his hands and slaps the dusty concrete. He swipes angrily at the ball. *Sure thing, buddy*. The funny thing is, a different me would've paid him a visit after the game and "borrowed" his sneakers.

I set my feet, twisting my shoes until I can hear the gravel crunch. I flip some stray hair out of my eyes. I jab step left and crossover right and he's toast, instantly in my rearview, nothing left of him but a whiff of Old Spice. The crowd starts spazzing, each *ooh* and *ahhh* and *órale* like a piece of Pop Secret. Later I might feel a little bad for the kid, getting embarrassed like that. But right now it's all business. I'm at home close to the rim, with all the trees, so when some big guy starts waving his branches, I squeeze an underhand pass to Justin, who's waiting in his sweet spot under the rim.

Justin lays it in off the backboard baby-soft. Ball game.

We win so much it's no big deal anymore. Forget the sweaty hugs, the jumping up and down, the yelling. That's amateur stuff you do when you think you're going to lose. That was the beginning of the summer, when we were just happy to lose by less than thirty, when we didn't even have jerseys. It ain't like that anymore. Now we show up and kick ass. Now we scare teams into staying home. Last week we had two games canceled because every kid on the other team conveniently had a sick *abuela* to take care of. "Some weird flu going around," they all lied. We haven't lost in forever, and after every game we shake hands, real cool, like we knew we were going to win all along.

Justin and I got a special handshake. It's hard to explain but it takes a full minute to finish and includes a part where we pretend to turn Super Saiyan.

"I couldn't even see you when I made that pass," I tell him.

"That's crazy," he says, smirking. "How do you pat yourself on the back with such short arms?"

I try to surprise him with a punch in the shoulder, but he shrugs it off and puts me in a headlock. I'm pinned against his chest, inhaling armpit fumes. Part of his jersey ends up in my mouth and I swallow a bunch of vinegary sweat. His biceps press against my throat. He's got a little meat on his bones now, I'll give him that. There was a time when he wouldn't even have dreamed of putting his hands on me. But now that he's got a girlfriend he's all grown up, real tough. I'm happy for him, I really am, but that doesn't stop me from winding up for a couple of kidney shots.

"Just say, 'Justin Shaw is better than me at everything and he gets more girls than I do' and I'll let go."

"Okay, okay," I say. "Justin Shaw is—" and as soon as he relaxes I elbow him in the gut. He bends over and groans like a tied-up dog.

Everybody's laughing. Sometimes it's scary to feel this good. I mean, we just won and the crowd's still buzzing and the sky's Crayola blue and there's an older girl in the crowd eyeing me and I got money in my pocket and I got no issues with nobody. The problem is that these moments never last. A fun fact about my life is that there's always some bullshit right around the corner. Always a fly in the soup. Life Lesson #508: If one thing is going really well, that just means something else is about to go really, really wrong. So I'm not even surprised when I see Officer Appleby, my court-appointed Community Mentor, politely squeezing his way through the crowd.

"All I can say," he says, shaking his head, "is wow. My goodness, what a game! What. A. Game! The way you passed! The way you dribbled!"

I can feel a bunch of eyes suddenly on us. A dark ring of sweat lines the collar of Officer Appleby's polo. The whole thing is starched cardboard-stiff. Officer Appleby's the least police-officer-looking police officer I've ever seen. Just looking at his wide-legged khakis makes me cringe.

He shakes everyone's hand. Officer Appleby doesn't take shaking hands lightly. The first time he came to see us play, he gave us all a lesson on it. Extra-firm grip, bold eye contact, confident nod. Let the other guy release first. A good handshake, he said, will open "many a door." He never did say which doors or where they went. Now, Justin and I have an "Appleby" part of our handshake routine where we squeeze each other's hand until we can feel our bones rubbing together and one of us quits.

As my Community Mentor, Officer Appleby's responsible for keeping tabs on me between 7:00 a.m. and 7:00 p.m. Every morning I have to text him and tell him about my daily plans. A couple of times a week we'll spend a few minutes talking about my feelings, about where my "disruptive behaviors" come from. If he's got a call in our neighborhood, he drops by to see what I'm up to. But it's not as bad as it seems. He never yells, not even when I lie and throw him off with a b.s. schedule. And sometimes he'll stop by for dinner and tell us about the funny calls he gets during the day: the guys trapped in the bathroom by their angry cats, the neighbors mad at each other for leaving their Christmas lights up too long. When we're done, he'll take everyone's plates to the sink, roll his sleeves up, and start scrubbing, even if Mamá protests.

"What?" Officer Appleby will say. "I can't hear you over the water. Let me finish these dishes first and then we'll talk."

Mamá will pout but stay seated. When you've been in the kind of trouble I've been in, the Officer Applebys of the world ain't too bad.

As I walk up my block I see; Mamá standing barefoot on the lawn, trying to smooth out the wrinkles in her pajamas. Her hair is all crazy-looking, a frizzy brown bun, a bird's nest. My spidey senses are tingling. Mamá can be a little weird—you should see her when she's painting—but she never steps out in nothing but the flyest. She'd die before she let the neighbors catch her without lipstick on. Wrapped around her leg is my kid brother, Tomás, also in his pajamas, his thumb stuck deep in his mouth. I'm still a couple of houses down when she waves me over.

"A bird's in the house!" she yells. Tomás buries his face in her leg. "Papi's trying to kill it!"

"Why don't he just open the windows?" I ask.

She tries to tuck a couple of stray strands into her bun but they fall right out. "Please, Frankie, just go help him. I can't work with no bird in the house."

When I get inside, curtains are blowing in the breeze like little ghosts. Papá is watching a baseball game.

"You need my help?" I ask.

"Oh," Papá laughs. "The bird? That was

forty-five minutes ago."

"You want me to tell her?"

Instead, he pats a seat on the couch. Most of the time Papá and I are butting heads. He wants me to stay at home and live slow, get in my books. He hates that I like being out doing my thing. But nowadays I'm trying to be better. Last time I was in youth court I could see the lines in Papá's face get deeper and deeper. And every time the judge spoke Papá looked like he was getting smaller and smaller. That surprised the hell out of me. I've seen Papá drop a cinder block on his foot and sing boleros on the way to the hospital. I never thought I was hurting him.

Now I sit to the left of him, just far enough away to give him some space. The right side is Papá's side; the seat is a smooth crater made by Papá's meteoric butt. The orange fabric smells like his cologne, Le Something of Something, stuff I sometimes sneak a few sprays of when I go out. The left side smells like fruity expensive lotion— that's Mamá's side. When I was a kid I only sat on Papá's side and would pretend that my forearms were as hairy as his, that my armpits sprouted hair like his, that my butt could make craters like his.

"You smell," Papá says. "You play some ball today?"

"Yeah," I say. "When you coming to a game?"

"I'm coming, I'm coming. Gotta find time."

"You ain't doing nothing right now."

He snorts. "You don't see me watching this game?"

The A's are losing so Papá's moody. That's one way we're alike—we're both poor sports. Blake strikes out Timmons and the TV shows the yellow-and-gold crowd clapping half-heartedly, roasting in the sun. Then they go to commercial. Papá pumps his fist and looks up, and it's like he's just noticing I'm there.

"So," he says. "You win or what?"

"We never lose."

One of Papá's eyebrows shoots up his forehead. "Is that right?"

"Never."

"Well, if I come, I might mess up your groove."

"Groove don't have nothing to do with it. We're just good."

He keeps his eyes on me. I know he's searching my face for a lie. "Okay, that's what I like to hear. I'm proud of you, Francisco. You've been good this summer. No messing up or nothing. You gotta keep that up."

I nod and start pulling at a thread in the cushion. Why am I suddenly embarrassed? Papá isn't known to be generous with the compliments. I want to tell him about the day I just had, how my assist led to the game-winner, but I don't—maybe the compliment well has run dry for the day. I stop pulling on the thread before he gets mad. We're watching the A's take their at-bats when Mamá storms back in.

"*Culero*," she says, dusting her feet off. "So I'm a joke to you? Do I look like a big joke?"

"I was just having a moment with my oldest son," Papá says, laughing. He hasn't taken his eyes off the TV. "*Mira*, Frank, tell her!"

Mamá stares at me. Behind her, Tomás is shaking his head, his eyes wide with fear. "Francisco," she says, "do not lie to me."

"It's true," I say, holding my hands up. "We were just talking."

"See?" Papá says, laughing even harder. I get all of my smoothness from him. He stands up, sweeps the hair off of Mamá's damp forehead, and kisses her between the eyebrows. He takes her by the hand and leads her to the couch. Before he sits her down, he sweeps the cushion off carefully, even though there's nothing there. He puts his arm around her and pulls her close, lets her smell him. When he turns and winks at me, I know it's my cue to exit.

"Okay," she says to me, sinking into Papá's shoulder. "Have your little fun. Be like your Papi. Make a joke of your poor mother."

Soon, I can hear them laughing from my bedroom.

Like I said, smooth.

Tomás and I sleep in the same back bedroom, in the same bed. At night our room glows: stickers of dinosaurs and hot air balloons turn the walls a pale green. We sleep on *Sesame Street*–themed covers that Mamá is too sappy to get rid of. Tomás is five and doesn't know he's spoiled rotten. Back in the day, when I was five, we didn't even have a microwave. I had three shirts I wore to school and barely any toys: I had to make forts for my toy soldiers out of old cereal boxes. Tomás gets everything he wants because my parents don't want him to turn out like me. Even though he's advanced enough to not wet the bed, he's nowhere close to becoming a man. That's what happens when you're spoiled—you don't know how to hustle. So I try to give him a little game each night before we go to bed, let him know what he's in for once he hits adulthood.

"When you get to be a man," I whisper, "you gotta show females you don't really care if they like you or not. That way they like you more."

Tomás makes a face and the green light makes him look sick. "I like everybody," he shouts, forgetting how to whisper. I pinch him and he remembers.

"*Like*, like," I say. "Like you wanna kiss them and hang out and stuff."

"That's gross."

"And you want to make sure that if you got a girlfriend, you always have a girl or two on the side. That way the girlfriend gets jealous and likes you even more."

Tomás yawns and pulls the sheets under his chin. "Tell me a story."

He's hopeless, but I don't have a choice. Without a story he won't go to sleep, meaning I'll have to listen to him recite animal facts all night. I worked in the library at a YA camp once, so I've got a million stories in my back pocket. If I'm in a bad mood, I'll frighten Tomás with a good one about flesh-eating ghosts, and when he falls asleep I pinch his shoulders until he runs to our parents' room and tries to sleep in their bed. But today's been a good day, and I'm feeling generous.

"Which one?" I ask.

"The one about how you stole the Batmobile."

I sigh. "You always want that one."

He pulls the covers over his head, but I know he's smiling. "It's my favorite."

"Everybody knows Batman," I say, "was just some dude lucky enough to be born rich. He ain't like us, Tomás. He ain't had to work for nothing. Don't even know the meaning of hard work. Probably got somebody to wipe his ass for him. So one day he tries to get at my lady, all slick—"

"And you told him to stop it."

"Right. 'Cause I ain't afraid of nobody. Life Lesson #367: Never be afraid of nobody. So I asked what Catwoman would think about all this. But Batman just keeps going. He says maybe your girl wants something a little different, something a little nicer. Big old stupid smile on his face. So I sock him in the nose right there, because you can't let nobody disrespect you, especially not in front of your girl—"

"And he starts crying!"

"Nobody ever thought to punch him in the nose. You do that with sharks, too: If you ever see a shark, you punch it in the nose. Now he's crying, holding his bloody nose, so I rip off his utility belt and stomp on it. All cheap stuff, because Batman gets his stuff made discount, in China. Look it up. Now it's just me and him, man to man, and of course he starts backing away, because he's nothing without his gadgets—"

Tomás squeals. "Is that when you stole the Batmobile?"

"I mean, what was I supposed to do? He left it running, open for the taking. Of course I hopped in. In my book, it would've been a crime not to hop in. I rode it around on the freeway for a while."

Right outside our window two cats start going at it, hissing until one runs through the bushes into the neighbor's yard. Then there's a long silence. "That really happened, Frankie?" Tomás asks.

I cross my arms behind my head and close my eyes. "Every word."

At first they thought it was ADHD. Mamá cried, thinking I was dying, not knowing the principal said that about every kid who acted up. They put me on Ritalin and every day for a year it felt like my muscles were going to bust out of my skin. Next it was dyslexia. A friendly lady who smiled and talked at the same time showed me a bunch of street signs. Stop sign, caution sign, that kind of thing. She wanted to know what I saw. I told her I saw the words, what the hell else was there to see? She packed her bag quickly. So, no dyslexia. Now they've settled on me being "emotionally troubled." I don't even know what that means, except that they think the cure for it is talking to Officer Appleby about my feelings for thirty minutes a few times a week.

"Tell me," Officer Appleby said the first time we met, "about the joyriding incident."

He leaned forward, one hand stroking his goatee. There wasn't much to tell. I was flunking eighth grade and had cut school to go see the new Star Wars. I was walking down Foothill Boulevard, and it just so happened that some guy ran into the liquor store and left his car running. And it just so happened that I wanted to know what it would be like to drive a Grand Am. So I did, and it would've been fine until I crashed into a hot-dog cart a couple of blocks away.

I leave that part out of the version I tell Tomás.

"So do you think you have an issue with impulse control?" Officer Appleby asked.

"No," I said, "I think I have an issue with liking nice cars."

That's how it is with us, always a back-and-forth. Officer Appleby tries to give me Adult Wisdom. I stick to my guns and come back with real talk. Once he dropped his voice real low, trying to sound all soothing, and asked why I hated school so much. Why did I throw erasers at kindly substitute teachers? Why did I feel it acceptable to come to school reeking of marijuana? I asked him to tell me what was so interesting about school. Learning stories about old dead white dudes who never did nothing for nobody but themselves? Not interested.

"Surely," Officer Appleby said, "Shakespeare is not merely some 'old, dead white dude.'"

Officer Appleby's the kind of person who thinks that everything you need to know comes from books. Every weekend he stars in a theater troupe called the Bleeding Hearts.

They do kid-friendly versions of Shakespeare. It wouldn't surprise me if he had a bronze *retablo* of Shakespeare, the way Mamá has one of her mother in that creepy corner of the living room.

"He is to me," I said.

He looked at me with one eyebrow cocked, like I was stupid. But I ain't no dummy. I know all kinds of facts. I know that there are no pain receptors in the brain. I know that Venus used to look a lot like Earth before its atmosphere fried. I know that California, Arizona, New Mexico, and Texas all used to be a part of Mexico. I know how to tie seven different kinds of knots. I know all kinds of stuff even if I do think school is b.s.

Today, Officer Appleby wants to know what nonviolent strategies I might use to resolve conflicts. My next fight could mean expulsion from the district. We're riding in his squad car through the neighborhood with the windows down. A smoky, barbecue-y breeze is blowing in. *Norteño* floats in from a party somewhere. On one block a bunch of kids with water guns chase each other across the street, the streams pinging the side of the car as we pass. On the next block two *viejos* look under the hood of an old Ford sitting on cinder blocks. Officer Appleby waves at them. They stand up straight and watch us pass before they bend over again.

"I don't have any strategies," I say.

"Here's another question: Do you consider your conflict resolution methods to be effective?"

"When I'm fighting? I mean, the conflict pretty much ends right there. That's effective to me."

We hit a stop sign and a stray dog jumps in front of the car. It just stands there in front of the bumper, working at an itch on its matted back. Officer Appleby waits, tapping his thumbs on the steering wheel. Anybody who's been in our neighborhood for five minutes knows that dog is blind as hell. He ain't moving. I reach over and honk the horn and it runs off.

"That's what I mean," Officer Appleby says. He's trying not to sound annoyed. "The difference between being patient and impatient."

"Patience would've had us sitting here all day like dumbasses."

"'Upon the heat and flame of thy distemper sprinkle cool patience.'" He flips his shades up, impressed with himself. "*Hamlet.*"

He turns the volume on the scanner

all the way down and every few seconds he clears his throat. I think he wants me to ask him how he handles conflict, so I ask.

"A very good question," he says brightly. "Little known fact about Shakespeare is that he was very antiwar, anti-conflict. He believed in carefully picking one's battles. For example: I would like a promotion at work. I have served capably for over ten years now and still no promotion. But am I going to come right out and ask for a promotion? Do I listen to my wife and storm into my boss's office, making ultimatums? No. That might make some very important people very mad. And maybe those people were just about to give me a promotion. And then where would my promotion be? Dead, that's where. DOA. So I will continue to work diligently and be patient and wait for my opportunity and be extra-prepared when it comes."

I stare out the window, at the dog wandering into the middle of another intersection. "How do you know it's coming?"

"It will come. They always come."

Coach Wise wants to know if we've ever heard of the word *complacent*.

"Any guesses?" he asks.

He blows his whistle and we're running again. Justin and Janae run together, slow and steady, their arms and legs in sync. Behind them, White Mike has started walking. His cheeks are fired up, lava red. Adrian puts a hand on his back, trying to push him forward, but it's no use. Mike's too big and Adrian's too small. I haven't been able to feel my legs for fifteen minutes. The sun killed all the clouds; we're getting deep-fried out here. When we finish we all crowd around a little bit of shade under the backboard, panting like dogs. It's been thirty minutes of this, punishment for a bad practice. Last time I was this tired I was hopping fences, running from some stoner who realized I was selling him dirt. But at least I was making money.

"Complacent means," I say, taking a deep breath, "that this running shit is for the birds."

It's true that we're out of shape, but I'm not a rabbit—I don't just run for no reason. I walk to the nearest tree and don't look back. In the shade the sweat on my back turns cool. I don't care about all the ants crawling over the bark. I close my eyes and lean against the trunk. It feels good here, better than good, and if my team had any sense they'd join me. Soon enough, White Mike walks over and lies down real slow next to me. He presses his cheeks into the dirt, first one side, then the other. Then everyone else comes, too.

"Well," Coach Wise says, tossing us water bottles, "I hope everyone has learned their lesson."

"Lesson?" I ask. My mouth is bone-dry but I don't pick up the water. "You gonna revive me when I get heat stroke?"

Coach Wise shakes his head. "I was trying to make a point about your effort level. It was bad today. You're developing bad habits."

"The only habit we got is winning. Focus on that habit."

Janae sits up. She splashes water on her face and pours some on Justin's head. "I agree that we do need to practice hard," she says diplomatically, "but I also agree that we might not have to practice this hard."

Now that Janae's spoken up, Justin has the courage to say something, too. "My vision was getting a little blurry for a second," he says, quickly taking a sip of water.

Coach Wise gulps down an entire bottle, as if he's done anything but blow his whistle. "You said you wanted to play inside, so we're getting ready to play inside. It's a different game."

"Basketball's basketball," I say. "Inside, outside, wherever. It don't become magic because the floor's different. You lace up your shoes and hoop."

Coach Wise shrugs. He says fine, he may not agree, but at the end of the day it's our team. He spends the next thirty minutes droning about strategy for our next game. I'm sure it's important, but I've got better things to do, like watch this ant run over my shoulder. It's making crazy zigzags, running for its life. Right before it gets back to the tree I smash it.

Papá said he's coming to my next game. He said so this afternoon, while I was helping him hook up our new TV. Mamá's mad at him for buying it. She walked right past him when she got home, didn't respond when he said hi. Papá couldn't care less. *Wait until Uncle Eddie sees it*, he said. *He's going to piss his pants!* I held it in place as he screwed it to the wall.

"You got it?" he asked.

"I got it," I said.

"You sure?"

I gripped the edges tighter. "I said I got it."

"Imagine the Raiders on this. Gonna be like we're there."

He grunted as he tightened a screw.

"Mamí will come around. Throw a nice horror flick on with a bunch of blood and she'll come around."

I watched him tighten the screws until they wouldn't turn any more. He held all the screws in his mouth, in his cheek, like he was chewing tobacco. When he wanted to put in a new screw, he held one in his teeth, sucked the spit off, and spit it into his hand.

"You said your game's inside, right?" he asked.

"Yeah," I said. "We're playing inside now. At the middle school. Just a scrimmage."

"Good. Playing inside will be good for you." He pointed his screwdriver at me. "You getting a little dark, Frankie."

I looked down at my arms. They looked regular, maybe a little browner than usual, but regular. I've always been darker than Papá, whose cheeks can turn red as White Mike's.

"The game's tomorrow," I said, ignoring Papá. "Five thirty."

He tightened one last screw and stepped back. He pulled me over and put his arm around me. We looked at our reflections in the screen. "Ain't you happy you got an old man who's good with his hands? Ain't you happy about that?"

I show up to the gym early, before the janitors have swept the dust off the floors. I take a couple of laps to loosen up, my shoes squeaking against the hardwood. It's strange-sounding and part of me starts to miss the sound of the concrete, the way the gravel crackles. Since I don't have a ball, I practice with an imaginary one, up and down the court, crossing over imaginary defenders and hitting imaginary lay-ups until I'm good and sweaty.

Slowly, the gym starts to fill. First, the janitors, who wipe down the floors. Then the ref shows up, a short guy who tucks his shirt deep into his shorts. By game time there's maybe twenty people in the stands, including Papá, who's in his work clothes, his shirt and jeans wrinkled because Mamá's still not talking to him. A couple of feet from him is Officer Appleby. They'll spend the whole game talking about my progress, how I've come so far this summer. Papá will laugh politely at his jokes, thinking he's just doing what it takes to keep me in Officer Appleby's good graces.

The other team huddles up at the other end of the court. They don't look like nothing special. Nobody who looks crazy fast or strong or big. Nothing to be worried about.

"Okay," Coach Wise says. "Just play our game. Do what you've been doing all summer."

"Winning time," I tell Justin. He daps me. I give Papá a thumbs-up and he gives me one back.

We win the tip. I get the ball, do my usual crossover and drive down the lane. I'm surrounded by three guys, so many hands and arms I can't see nothing. I try to pass the ball out to Justin but it's intercepted and they get an easy two. That's my bad. The next time down, I pass it to Janae on the wing, but they close out on her quick, like they know she likes to catch and shoot. Janae's not great going to the basket, so the ball gets poked away. Another fast break, another two points. Coach Wise folds his arms across his chest. I look up at Papá and he's tipped his head to the side, the way he does when he can't believe the A's have given up a late-inning homer.

The whole game is like this. They trap me at half-court and force me to throw the ball into the stands. Coming down the lane is like being inside a carwash. I turn around and around looking for someone to pass to. We do our usual passing and cutting, and they pick off the passes like they know what's coming. Coach Wise screams at us, the veins in his neck turning into big ropes. He begs us to find our Zen, to play harder. On defense we get lost behind screens we don't even see coming. We lose our men running through a maze of bodies and back cuts. I get called for three fouls in the first five minutes.

"That's not a foul," I tell the ref.

He shrugs. "In streetball it ain't. In here it is."

At halftime we're down by twenty-five. I look at Justin, who keeps looking at the scoreboard like they got something wrong.

"Damn," I say.

"We can always come back," he says weakly. He doesn't even believe that.

We've got no chance, not even when the other team puts their subs in. We get nothing clean or easy. I get called for carrying. ("Streetball move," the ref says. "Illegal.") Instead of handing the ball to the ref I kick it into the stands and get ejected. Coach Wise begs the ref to let me stay in the game. What's the point? Janae gets her shots blocked. Justin and White Mike miss bunnies. I'm watching the clock, wishing it would speed up. I don't look up at Papá. I'm too scared to see the look on his face.

The buzzer puts us out of our misery. We've lost by thirty.

We huddle in a spot under the bleachers. I look at the grimy floor, at the wrappers and empty cups that slipped through from above. Out on the court the other team does a victory chant. Above us, their parents talk about us, how streetballers always get smoked when they play teams with any kind of organization.

"At least we kept the second half close," White Mike says. "That, I would say, shows some heart."

Coach Wise taps a pen in the palm of his hand. "I'm not one to say I told you so," he says, "but I did tell you that indoor competition is much tougher. I did say that."

"Maybe we should stick to playing

outside," Justin says.

"Maybe," I whisper.

"Jesus," Coach Wise says, rolling his eyes. "Is somebody dead? Did somebody die out there? You got your butts kicked and now your feelings are hurt. If you still want to play, meet me on the blacktop tomorrow."

We return to the court silently, eyes down. Officer Appleby is waiting for me.

"Well," he says. He struggles to keep a smile on. "That certainly was something, wasn't it?"

"You don't gotta be nice," I say.

"That certainly was something."

Papá's waiting for me in the parking lot. I throw my bag into the back and hop in the front. I lean against the window and close my eyes. If Papá says anything right now, I might lose it. But instead he pats me on the shoulder. On the way up Bancroft I listen to the whining of his Chevelle, the clinking when he brakes hard. When we stop, the car bucks and kicks like a bull. It's a nice car to look at but the engine's rotten. Mamá wanted to use the TV money to get something more reliable, but the way Papá looks, with his arm hanging out the side—he was never going to give this car up.

The whole ride we don't speak. When we pull into the driveway, he throws the car in park and leaves the engine running.

"Frankie," he says, patting my leg, "I still think you're doing pretty good."

A knot the size of a tennis ball sits

in my throat. My eyes start to sting. I get out of the car and slam the door. I'm more surprised than hurt. Papá's been angry, confused, and disappointed with me before. He's taken me on walks after Mass and told me I needed to do better. He's sat next to me in the principal's office and called me an embarrassment.

But he's never, ever shown me pity.

The night I got locked up for joyriding I slept like a baby, knocked out as soon as I got home. Woke up the next morning like nothing had happened and clammed up when Mamá tried to talk about it. Officer Appleby says that's one of my problems, that I take no time to reflect, that I don't see the thread running between the past and present. I bet he'd be thrilled to know that tonight is different. My mind keeps hitting rewind. Every time I close my eyes I see the forest of arms, feel them wrapping around me and squeezing like vines. I throw the covers off and sit up, suddenly hot.

Tomás is crazy with energy. He sits next to the window and tries to pinch the full moon between his sticky fingertips. The whole room smells like gummy bears. He keeps asking why the moon is white. Why isn't it gold, like the sun? And do I think he can jump to the moon? And why do fingernails look like the moon? And why do fingernails grow? Why, why, why?

"If you don't shut up," I whisper.

"You've got to be patient and keep your eye on the prize," he says.

That's Mamá talking. Tomás likes to repeat things he hears her say. I'm doing everyting I can to resist the urge to smack him.

"Shut up," I say. "I'm telling you to shut up."

"Saying *shut up* hurts you more than the person you say it to."

"Stop repeating things Mamá says."

Nowadays Mamá hands out wisdom like de la Rosas. She's happy, so she's painting more: An unfinished portrait of the hills blocks out a window in the living room. She stands there in a big white T-shirt, mixing buckets of pinks and silvers and oranges, biting her top lip.

She wants to get the burned parts right, the way the black and gold mix together. I've seen her just stand there for an hour, not moving except to mix the paint a little. Around the house she's made big mounds of things: beans, cans, loose change, rolls of toilet paper, pillows, shoes. You'll spend a whole day looking for the remote before you realize it's buried under a hill of phone chargers. But soon she'll throw some white paint over the whole thing and start over. She might do fifty of them before she gets it right, but she says that's the cost of love.

I don't want any part of love, then. Sometimes I've seen her in these funks when she can't get the eyes right on some *vieja* so all she does is drink Folgers and rearrange the candles and old photos on her altar, moving one thing an inch to the left and then an inch to the right, so much moving that it looks like when she started. "*M'hijo*, I'm lost," she'll say. "Completely lost." She'll lie on the couch, her eyes shut tight because she's seeing the *vieja* everywhere, in spilled salt, on shower tiles. Even Papá will be on his best behavior. He'll warn us to stay away, that we can expect a slap to the back of our heads if we get within sniffing distance of her. Days and days she'll go without eating or changing her clothes.

"You're like your mother," Papá once told me. I shook my head thinking it was just another one of his cryptic sayings. Mamá's mother was a painter, and Mamá's mother's mother painted Myrtle

Gonzalez's official portrait. I'm supposed to be like Papá, gold chain peeking out from my collar, talking out of the side of my mouth, enough game to charm a snake.

# CHAPTER 4
# EMERGENCY

We have a play-in game at JamLand in a few weeks. If we win, we're in an indoor league for the rest of the summer. Sponsorships, shoes, the whole nine. We'd never have to worry about gear again, or some fools snatching our court. Maybe a game on local access every now and then.

Coach Wise says this kind of opportunity doesn't come around all that often. All morning we've been running up Cleveland Cascade, one miserable, crumbling step after another, until we get to the top. On nice days there's a sweet view of Lake Merritt, all the glittering traffic and silvery water and the playground and the fountain and the dog walkers and the little foot-powered boats. It's usually real pretty, except today I'm hunched over, breathing in big gulps of cool, stinging air, trying not to throw up. Somehow we seem to run way more than we hoop. I must've told Coach Wise a thousand times that this ain't a track team. I stand up to shoot him a dirty look.

"Perhaps you should've looked at the last team like that!" he says. He makes a big show of taking a deep gulp of fresh air and blows his stupid whistle.

We run in a line down the steps, past the dog walkers and joggers and pairs of chatty old ladies. You have to look out for the people but you can't forget about the branches and rocks in the path, either. The stairs are tiny, just big enough for a single foot. It takes a whole lot of finesse: One misstep and you'll go face-first into a slab of concrete. But the end is in sight, one last flight. I try to speed up to get things over with when something catches my foot. Suddenly I'm at the bottom of the stairs and my whole body is aching, especially my ankle. My ankle: It feels like someone's holding a hot knife to it, stabbing it in a thousand places. Bolts of fire shoot up my leg when I move it even a little. I don't realize I'm biting my lip until I taste the blood in my mouth. The whole team surrounds me, saying things I can't hear.

Everything that happens next is a blur: Coach Wise and Justin carrying me; my ankle hanging out of a truck window; my head in Janae's lap, her wiping the sweat off of my face with her shirt. Then we're in an emergency room, where it's so packed there's only one seat left, next to a guy with a bloody bandage wrapped around his throat. He smokes the butt of a cigarette and blows the smoke into his shirt. An angry nurse keeps coming over to tell him he has to put it out.

"Doesn't even hurt," he says, pointing to his bandage. "Looks worse than it is."

He looks down at my ankle. It's the size of a football, with blue and purple bruising around the bone. He asks how I hurt it.

I motion like I'm shooting a jumper.

"You? Basketball?" He laughs so hard that the bloody bandage around his neck starts to slip off. "You see something new every day."

An hour later the nurse says it's a sprain, wraps it up in a bandage, and sends me on my way with some ice and Advil.

"Looks pretty gnarly," she says, eyeing the bruise admiringly. Her shirt is covered in happy-face stickers. After she wraps my ankle, she grabs a Sharpie and draws a smiley face on the tape. "Needs two or three weeks, at least."

"Three weeks?"

"You saw that bruising? That's your ligament saying 'I've been stretched beyond my usual range of motion! Please rest me so I can be happy!' Have a nice day!"

I've been lying in Papá's spot on the couch,

my foot propped on a stack of old pillows. When you're hurt or sick in this house, everyone has to be nice to you. Those are the rules. Mamá makes sure I always have some ice packs nearby and rewraps my ankle every morning before she starts painting. Papá jokes about all the times he milked an injury to get out of pulling weeds in the summer. It kills him that I'm hogging his new TV to play video games, but he can't say anything. Tomás follows me when I get up to go to the bathroom. He pretends to limp, his whole leg wrapped mummy-style in toilet paper. The way they're treating me, I'm thinking I should get hurt more often.

It's amazing how much people can talk when they know you got to listen. Every few days the team comes by with news. When

Coach Wise isn't here, they sit on the floor and pick at the rug and complain about him, how he's running them to death and he takes everything too seriously. When Coach Wise comes alone, he complains about *them*, how they're not taking the challenges of indoor ball seriously.

And then Officer Appleby stops in with a gift.

"Frank," he says, "my opinion is always: Once one door closes, another opens. While you may be out of commission basketball-wise, you're still free to develop other skills."

It's a journal. The front cover has a pen dripping tiny drops of ink. Inside the front cover it says THERE IS NO GREATER AGONY THAN BEARING AN UNTOLD STORY INSIDE YOU. Jesus.

I ask him what I'm supposed to do with it, since school's out and I have no writing assignments.

"Use it to spend some quality time with yourself," Officer Appleby says. He pulls out a matching journal and flips through pages full of neat cursive. "Learn how to notice things. Tell stories. Write jokes. Or secrets. Write letters to your friends. Whatever your heart desires." He says he'll be checking my progress every few days, just to see if I'm doing things right.

He wants me to notice things? When you're trying to walk out of the Apple Store with an iPhone at the bottom of your backpack, you learn how to notice things real fast. I'm already a pro at that.

# Journal #1

I don't know what to write. My favorite food is pistachio gelato. My favorite movie is Scarface because that's a dude who's about his money. My favorite color is green. My favorite subject is math. My favorite animal is the whale shark.

I hate crabs, Pokémon, and people who talk with their hands.

Justin Shaw is my best friend. He's known me the longest. We got secrets I wouldn't even write here.

Nobody thinks I have deep thoughts, but I do. The judge in my last case barely even looked at me. Didn't even hear me out. He said I've shown a "pattern of stupid decision making" so it was no surprise that

I was standing there in front of him. He basically called me stupid. Like I never got an A in math or "mugwump" on Jeopardy! before.

People think that because they got a position that's higher than yours they're better than you. That's what gets me the most. I'm supposed to bow down to somebody just because they got a position? They never made no mistakes? Their shit don't stink?

I want to get rich. If I was rich, I wouldn't even spend all the money on myself. The first few things, yeah, of course: nice house, nice car that could become a boat or submarine. But after that I'd help everybody else out. I'd get Mamá a house just for her paintings. I'd get Papá a new muscle car with real brakes. I'd get Tomás his OWN bed!!! The whole team would get new uniforms and we'd always fly private jets to games and we'd only eat at Olive Garden. Not to mention women galore. Little robots that did your chores for you. Everybody would be living good, and when somebody needed something I'd take care of it, no problem. All they'd have to promise is that they'd have my back if something happened. That's the most important thing to me--loyalty. If you don't have loyalty, you don't have nothing. Doesn't matter how much money you have.

Running out of ideas now. I'm good at telling stories, so maybe I'll write one. Tomás eats my stories up, even the bad ones. For example, that Batman story is crappy but he loves it. I got stories way better than that. Maybe I'll try something new. Sci-fi or Western. Ever since I saw

Gattaca I've been wanting to write a sci-fi story. What I won't write is no love story. That's not what I do. And what if this thing got into the wrong hands? Now the whole world knows Frank Torres writes love stories in his journal like a girl? Never gonna happen.

# CHAPTER 5

# THE NEW MONA LISA

Mamá wants to ask a favor. I can tell. She's been laying the *m'hijo*s on thick all morning and just now put a steaming mug of hot chocolate in front of me, marshmallows bobbing on the top just the way I like it. She put Tomás on time-out for watching cartoons while I was trying to sleep. That's never happened before. Now she's sitting on a small sliver of couch next to my head, tucking my blanket around my shoulders.

"*M'hijo*, could you do me a favor?" she asks sweetly.

"I knew it," I say. I can hear Tomás crying softly in our room. "Tomás never gets in trouble."

She tilts her head up and listens to him cry for a moment. "Tomás is fine. Can you do me this favor, *m'hijo*?"

"What is it?"

"I want you to agree before I tell you."

She adjusts my pillows and runs one of her hands through my hair. Blotches of dark paint dot her fingertips. Mamá has never stopped thinking of me as a five-year-old. I can do no wrong with her, and somehow this makes me feel guilty, even when I've done nothing wrong.

"Fine," I say.

"I want you to be in a painting."

I stare at her, waiting for the joke. "Me? What happened to your hills painting?"

"*M'hijo*, I won't be the one painting. I have a student."

Since I'm not doing anything, she says, I'd be a perfect stationary subject for one of her beginner students.

"Nah," I say. "I don't want nobody drawing my picture and having me out here looking crazy."

"Frankie, she's so talented! You won't look crazy, I promise. She just needs practice."

"She?"

Mamá's eyes narrow. She holds my nose between her fingers like the olden days and squeezes. "Frankie, I want you to promise you'll be on your best behavior. *Di* me. Promise me you'll let her do her work."

"Fine," I say. Like the olden days, we shake on it.

# Journal #2

Ankle is starting to feel better.
I hobbled to the bathroom and didn't
want to die. Looked in the mirror and
my eyes were red from too much TV.
Don't want this girl thinking I've got
pinkeye or something, so no more TV
for me.

I miss basketball more than
I thought I would. I thought I'd
miss the crowds and the girls but
I mostly miss my friends. Losing
sucked but at least we were losing
together. Too cheesy?

I've been kinda feeling low lately.
Usually I would tell Justin, but me
and Justin are going in opposite
directions. Justin is tall and has a
girlfriend. I have no girl plus a bum
ankle. It's like: I want to call him,

but if I call him and admit I'm not doing good that would be admitting I'm the loser in the relationship. But if I don't call him, maybe he'll think I don't want to be friends anymore? I don't know.

Mamá is very good about keeping her altar neat. She checks on it all the time and changes the veladoras as soon as the candle burns past halfway. We haven't gone to Mass in a while but I'm not complaining. Mass feels like school except everyone you know has to wear a collared shirt and act like they've never farted before.

Do art chicks like leather jackets? I was watching Breakfast Club. I think art chicks like sensitive guys, guys with lip rings. Do art chicks like guys who play basketball?

Do art chicks like guys that are hurt? Because they look sensitive? Every time Papá comes home with an aching back, Mamá is nicer. Not calling Mamá an "art chick," but just saying.

# CHAPTER 6
# NO NEW FRIENDS

Her name's Toni. Typical art chick who thinks she's some special misunderstood unicorn. Green swoop of hair that covers her eyes, nose ring, studded belt, studded bracelets, black shirt, black jeans, black shoes, black nail polish. Barely says a word. The type of chick who smokes cigarettes just so everyone will beg her to quit.

When she walked in with Mamá, I turned the TV on and tried to play it cool. But one look at her and I felt stupid about how I'd hurried to cut my toenails, gel my hair, and brush my teeth (twice) before she got here. My whole routine wasted. You don't need to break out the big guns for a girl like this. She set up her easel and a little table for her pencils and brushes. She opened the window to air the room out (I put on a bunch of Papá's cologne). Now she's just standing there, looking at me. It would be one thing if she was batting her eyelashes, the way girls like to do. But I feel like she's trying to look inside me. Everybody's always trying to look inside me—Officer Appleby, Papá, every assistant principal and school counselor I've ever had, everybody. Did anyone ever think that maybe I don't want them knowing what's going on in my soul?

"Excuse me," she says. "Can you take that jacket off?"

"My leather jacket?" I ask.

"Yeah, it's in the way."

Oh.

She's been sketching me for two hours, sitting with her back straight, her pencil making quick scratching sounds across the large pad. I'm annoyed. She doesn't care that I'm ignoring her. It's like she thinks I'm a piece of furniture, a part of the couch.

"Diego Rivera's my favorite artist," I say. Actually he's one of Mamá's favorites. "I really like the way he drew people."

"He didn't 'draw' 'people,'" she says, not looking up. "He painted. And the people he painted were peasants. Poor people. Folks everybody else forgot about."

"That's what I meant."

"That's not what you meant. If you meant it you would've said it."

She thinks she's so smart and so much better than everybody. I've been around girls like her before. You just have to show them you're smart, too, and they come right down off their high horse. So I put the news on and they're talking about a school closing down the street.

"That school sucked anyway," I say. "I never learned nothing there."

"Maybe," she says, "it would've sucked less if there was money for books. Or if the buildings weren't falling apart. Or they paid teachers better. Or they stopped building liquor stores across the street. Or they taught about Dolores Huerta and Richard Aoki."

You could sweep up all the names she drops. Every conversation is like that. I say something and she gives me a lecture, waving her paintbrush in the air like a gavel. That is how she talks, like a PBS special. She's so stuck up and she doesn't even know it. I can't figure out what Mamá sees in her.

# Journal #3

Toni is this girl who thinks she's the only person in the world who can draw. You don't have to be all sad and gloomy to draw. Here's this:

"Do you trust me?" Officer Appleby asks.

"Should I?"

He's looking out our living room window and into our neighbor's yard. Ms. Nuñez is back there putting wiring up around a tomato bush with her daughter, Vanessa. Ms. Nuñez can garden, straight up. They've got an apple tree, too, and sometimes it drops rotting apples into our yard—really good for throwing at your kid brother. It used to be that they'd bring empanadas over on Sundays and Vanessa

and Tomás would play tag and Ms. Nuñez
and Mamá would laugh about all the *chisme*
in the neighborhood. Now they don't talk
to us. Mamá thinks it's because we've got a
cop at our house all the time.

"Do you trust that I'm steering you
in the right direction? That I'm looking
out for your best interests?" Officer
Appleby asks.

That's how he's sounded since he got
here. Real businesslike, like he's never met
me before. It's making me nervous. I shift
so that I can sit up and get a better look at
him. His eyes are baggy and red. He wrings
his hands and wipes them on his pants.
Earlier, he leafed through the pages of
my journal quickly, chewing his pen cap
and looking disappointed.

Now he turns back to the window, to Ms. Nuñez. She looks up at us, and when she sees Officer Appleby she grabs Vanessa's hand and goes inside.

"Are those nice people over there?" he asks, pointing.

"Don't know them," I say.

"Sure." He shoves his hands in his pockets. "Everybody wants to keep secrets."

There's a cop show on TV. In this episode, a kid goes missing, and the TV detectives are chasing the school principal down a back alley. The cops all have chiseled jaws and their veiny biceps bust out of their tiny uniforms. When they catch the principal, they start talking in punch lines, like TV cops do. They tell him he's going to "detention." Officer

Appleby rolls his eyes.

"You know," Officer Appleby says, "I went to school, unlike a lot of these guys. But I thought: I'm gonna work my way up, not take any special favors. Be one of them."

I keep my eyes on the TV.

"Some guy in my class got promoted because of a bust he just walked into," he says. "Routine traffic stop and he found a truckload of real bad stuff."

He stands in front of the TV, blocking my view.

"Do I think he's a better cop than me?" he asks. "No. I know he doesn't put the work in that I put in. The hours."

Now he stands over me, so close that I can see the scabs under his chin where he cut himself shaving.

"It's just that if I had some kind of information that might help me do my job better and take it to the criminal element, or if someone pointed me in the right direction I could take it from there. That would be all I needed."

It takes me a second to understand what Officer Appleby wants, but before I can say anything his phone rings.

"Chief Myers!" Officer Appleby exclaims. His voice is suddenly high-pitched and ridiculous. "Yes, sir—Absolutely, sir—Excellent joke, sir!—No sir, wasn't doing anything at all—Always a pleasure to help you, sir, I'll be right on my way!"

He hangs up and puffs his chest out. "You have to sound professional when talking to your superiors."

"Very professional," I agree.

He sighs. His chest collapses like a flattened ball. "Well, just keep writing."

# CHAPTER 9
# WHO ARE YOU?

The dogs on my block go crazy when Toni walks down the street. She must look like an alien to them. She's over again wearing her usual black, sitting in her usual spot on the opposite side of the living room. Honestly, I'm feeling a little crazy myself. I don't like her at all, not even a little bit—so I'm not sure why I felt giddy when I opened the door for her. Why I couldn't stop thinking about her this morning before she came over? I can't even pretend to watch TV today. She sets up her easel slowly and unzips the bag she carries her canvas in. She lays out her pencils and brushes and paints gently. She reminds me of a mother, the way she touches things. Mamá used to hold Tomás like that, like he'd break into a million pieces if she was too rough. Toni sits in a little square of morning light and starts sketching.

"You'd be a lot prettier if you didn't wear black all the time," I say.

It's a long time before she says anything back. "Who are you to tell me what I should wear?"

"I was trying to give you a compliment."

"That's not a compliment."

The jersey I'm wearing is a throwback I put on for her, hoping she'd say something. It's green and white and I've gotten lucky every time I've worn it. She hasn't even noticed. Now it feels childish, like something Tomás would wear. Somehow, everything I do feels like the wrong thing. My face feels too brown, my legs feel too short, my jokes feel too stupid. Yesterday I made a joke about Mamá's breath that's worked a million times before but when Toni didn't laugh I wanted to disappear into a black hole.

In the afternoon Mamá comes to check on us. Tomás is wrapped around her leg, sucking his thumb as usual.

"How are you, Toni?" Mamá asks. "Is there anything you need? Is Frankie bugging you?"

"I'm fine," she says, looking at me. "We're good."

Tomás takes his thumb out of his mouth and stands next to me. He holds his arms straight in front of him like Harry Potter. Since he saw the movie he's been going around casting spells on everybody. I start to feel something heavy twist in my stomach.

"Did you tell her you have other girlfriends?" Tomás says.

Toni doesn't look up from the canvas so I can't tell if she heard or not. If Mamá weren't here I'd wipe the smile right off of Tomás's face. "Get out of here," I say. I remind myself to laugh. "You always say stupid things." I turn to Toni. "He always says stupid things."

"You said that if you want a girl to like you, you have to tell her you have a bunch of girlfriends. If that doesn't work I can cast a charm spell on her!"

I stare at him so hard he rewraps himself around Mamá's leg.

As soon as Mamá leaves, I change the subject.

"So, have you always been creative?" I ask.

"I like writing, I like drawing," Toni says. "Your mom got me into painting."

"So, it helps you with stress or what? I think that's why she does it."

"No, but I don't know how to explain it so you'd get it. It's like when everything you have inside needs to get out right now and there's only one way to let it out that feels good."

"Oh, like basketball."

She peeks around the easel. Her lips are pressed together tight. "No, not like basketball."

"Yeah, for me it is. It's like when I'm playing, nobody gets to judge me. No one gets to tell me nothing. And even if I mess up, no one's going to tell me I ruined my life. I can be mad or happy or sad and it's all good. I'm just free."

Toni's pencil scratches the canvas.

"So," I say, "we're both artists."

She stops sketching and peeks around the easel again. "No. We're not."

"Yes we are." I can tell she's a little angry and for some reason this makes me feel good. "I'll bet you I could do your art before you do mine."

"Basketball isn't art."

"How about this. If I write a story, you gotta come hoop with me."

Sure, this bet isn't fair. She doesn't know that I know a million stories anyway. But I'll feel guilty about that some other time.

"Huh?" she asks. "Aren't you hurt?"

I stand up and do a jumping jack. "All better."

Officer Appleby surprises me tonight. He usually doesn't come two days in a row. We sit outside, on the front steps. The crickets shout whiny, annoying songs. It's cool, almost cold, but Officer Appleby's forehead is sweaty. I keep looking inside, hoping Papá or Mamá will call me in for something, anything. He flips through my journal again, pausing on the drawing.

"Who is this?" he asks.

"That's me," I say.

"Oh." Officer Appleby's shoulders slump. He wipes his forehead. "Frank, I think I was being a little too indirect the other day. I want to be clear. A relationship is a two-way street. It requires that both parties enter into a mutually beneficial relationship. I have treated you kindly, have I not?"

I don't know where he's going with this, but I nod.

"I've been good to you," Officer Appleby continues. "For that, I expect cooperation. Shakespeare wrote that a friend should bear another friend's infirmities. Specifically, I expect to get information from you about what's going on in the neighborhood. Any kinds of"—he uses his fingers to make air quotes—"'activities.' That way, everybody wins. I look good and you stay out of court. Frank, as of right now, I do not think you are holding up your end of the bargain."

"So you want me to tell you about 'activities.' Meaning rat people out."

"Well, now you're putting words in my mouth."

"What makes you think I even know people involved in 'activities'?"

Officer Appleby smiles sadly. "Who are we kidding here, Frank? You do bad things. You want me to believe you don't know other people also doing bad things?"

I open my mouth but nothing comes out. A weird, painful pulsing starts behind my eyes. All the times I suckered kids and I never knew what it felt like until right now. Five minutes ago Officer Appleby put Tomás on his back and crawled across the floor like a wild stallion. Now this. I don't know which Appleby to believe. I can't tell which one is the real one.

## Journal #4

The Ventrilian War raged for a thousand years before anyone on Earth noticed. It's true that the war was originally fought two light-years away, in galaxies too dark and distant for the human eye, but the signs were all there. Rubble from the battles, what humans call "space rocks," had been falling onto Earth for centuries, where they were put in cold museums or kept in cardboard boxes by curious children. Battles were waged by throwing superheated balls of gas--on Earth those were called "shooting stars." Everything humans needed to know was around them, and when the last ship left Earth, and the last people born on Earth looked back out of the windows and saw every ocean burning, they knew they only had themselves to blame.

There had been hope at one point, before mankind went mad and turned on itself. It was no surprise that this happened, since humans are known around the galaxy for their capacity for blood. Their brains are simply not as developed as other galactic life forms. But early on there was hope. Two children had stumbled upon a discovery. Their names were Jank and Moni. They were opposites, so it'd be easy to assume they were natural enemies. Moni was cruel. She didn't like being nice to people. She got good grades in school, but she was also a kind of know-it-all, and there was no evidence that she had friends of any kind. On the other hand, Jank was loved in the small town they lived in. He may have been a little short for his age but that didn't stop him from being popular. He was captain of the local football team. Oftentimes his mother had to stand in the yard with a broom to keep his admirers at bay. What Jank saw in Moni the universe may never know, but without these two lovers, no one from mankind would've survived.

"Jank and Moni?" Toni asks.

"What?" I say.

"That's terrible." She tries to hide a laugh. "You really think I have no friends?"

"No, that's Moni."

"Right, right. *Moni.*"

"So you like it. I can tell you like it."

She reads the story again, shaking her head occasionally. "I said it's not bad. I'm not saying it's good, either."

She is sitting on the floor below her easel, drawing little skeletons on her hand.

For the first time she's taken her boots off. She has these little black feet that squirt around the carpet like worms. Why do I get so excited when I learn something new about her? Yesterday she let me wash a couple of her brushes in the sink. I held the brushes under the warm water and wondered what it might feel like if she ran her hands through my hair. I can't even help it. I'm lost in the sauce. I've been daydreaming about her more and more now that the painting's almost done.

"So," I say, "I guess you're coming with me to practice."

She groans. "I'm so out of shape. I actually used to play. I wasn't going to tell you."

I give her this look. Is this girl for real?

It's like she reads my mind. "For real.

But I stopped having time."

I nudge her in the ribs. "It's all good. I'll show you how to dunk."

She laughs. It's loud, the kind of laugh that makes you feel a lot funnier than you are. She tries to cover it with her hand and glances at me, waiting for me to say something.

"You don't like your own laugh?" I ask.

"Not really," she says.

"Your own laugh that you were born with?"

"Help me wash a couple brushes."

She walks over to the sink. This side of her is new, too, the side that won't say what she really thinks. But something tells me not to push it. I get up and help her.

"No," Coach Wise says. He's dragged me over to the water fountains so we can talk in private. "We have enough players."

"No we don't," I say. "We could use a sub so we can get rest."

Toni is standing with Janae, trying to dribble the ball between her legs. She's doing a pretty good job, even with combat boots on.

"Then I will find us a sub," Coach Wise says.

I fold my arms. "If she's not on the team, I'm not on the team."

Coach Wise growls. "I can't even—after everything we've—you want to ruin this for a—" He stomps back toward the court and blows his whistle.

I didn't mean for it to be like this. But

since Toni finished her painting there was a chance I'd never see her again. That's what she does to me—she makes me sound all dramatic. But at the end of the day, I can hang out with her if she's on the team. Everything else we can worry about later.

During dribbling drills, Justin wants to know if she's my new girl.

"Yeah," I say. "No. Maybe."

I don't know with Toni. She's the biggest puzzle I've ever encountered. She's decent at ball and agrees to come to practices and join Team Blacktop. She laughs at my jokes now, at the stories I tell about cutting school to chase geese at the park. She listens when I tell her my dreams, the plans I have for my future millions. She even showed me a corner of her painting the other day, the part with my foot propped up on a bunch of pillows. It's way prettier than my foot actually is. But she's never tried to hold my hand. She doesn't play with her hair when we're talking. Whenever I give her a long look, the thing everyone knows is supposed to lead to a kiss, she looks away. Today we walked under the Kissing Tree. It's got a heart-shaped trunk and the leaves make a soft shushing sound when you walk under them. I've kissed a million girls under here. But when we walked under it, and I told Toni it was the Kissing Tree, she peeled some of the bark off and said it was actually a chestnut. "An invasive species."

Am I doing something wrong here or what?

## Journal #5

Jank and Moni had history. They grew up on neighboring farms, in a small town on the outskirts of the badlands. They both rode horses and oftentimes they placed first and second in the county jumping shows. One day, they were riding out near the badlands at dusk when they stumbled upon a small metallic boulder. It was smoldering, too hot to touch. Jank, being the brave one, took his shirt off and tried to pick it up. It immediately sprang to life and spoke in a harsh metallic voice: "WHICHEVER TWO PEOPLE FIND THIS MESSAGE MUST AGREE TO BE TOGETHER FOR LIFE OR EARTH WILL BE DESTROYED." The pod shut, grew very bright, and vanished into itself.

Jank and Moni looked at each other.

Be together? Jank asked.
You and me? Moni asked.

They didn't know then that
they were Earth's last chance. They
didn't know that a hundred million
alien ships were descending from all
corners of the universe on the planet
as they spoke. And they didn't know
yet that the only reason anyone on
Earth would survive was because of
their love.

I guess we have to be together,
said Jank.
I don't know, said Moni.
We have to do it for the
universe, said Jank.
What if this is all just a big
misunderstanding? said Moni.

They rode back to their farms
and spent the night in the barn,
talking. They were just kids, fifteen

years old, not even old enough for a license. And now they had to save the world. Moni started crying and Jank held her in his big, strong arms. They looked up through the skylight of the barn and saw the distant lights of the spaceships descending.

That's when they decided that it was their duty to fall in love, that they would do it for the rest of humanity.

I think I love you, Jank said.
I think I love you, too, Moni said.

Toni's scratching her head. "I just don't get why the aliens would want them to be together."

"That's the mysterious part," I say. "I'll get to that later. The important thing is that they're together."

"And also isn't this the plot of that one Will Smith movie?"

"I'll fix that."

We're sitting in the backyard, watching waves of long grass go flat in the breeze. Actually, I'm watching Toni's mouth. I like watching the words form on her lips. Sometimes I'm so focused I actually miss what she's saying.

You know how you can talk to someone about everything and nothing at the same time? We look out at the grass or up at the clouds and just say whatever pops into our heads. She's a vegetarian, she goes to an art school during the year, she can burp the alphabet. She can't pronounce the word "sarcophagus." She got her period when she was eleven but didn't tell anyone until she was thirteen. These are things she never tells anybody, she says. I tell her about the fights, the joyriding, the teachers I've made cry. But it's not like before, when I said this stuff to impress girls. Now it's just another thing we talk about. It feels like something special, something real, with just the two of us sitting there and clouds like spaceships overhead, but when I lean in for the kiss, she pulls back.

"I thought you were feeling me," I say quickly.

"I mean, yes, I think you're cool," she says.

"Well?"

Toni sighs. "This always happens."

I'm confused. I wait for her to say something, and when she doesn't I nudge her.

"It's not that I don't like you. But this always—I'm always—I never know what to do."

When I look up for something to say,

the clouds look like chopped off heads.

"Every dumb movie," Toni says, "when a girl gets close to a guy, she's supposed to feel a certain way, do certain kinds of things. But every time I try to feel that way it doesn't work. I've tried and tried and it never works."

"Maybe it was something I did?"

I start thinking of all the things wrong with me: My eyes are too far apart, my feet are too big for my body, I sleep in the same bed as my kid brother, I got a record a mile long, I don't speak very good Spanish, I write stupid stories—

"It's not you, Frank," she says, "it's not."

She exhales hard. I've tried everything with this girl, everything I've watched Papá do, everything that's worked in the past, everything I can remember from the movies.

"Maybe it's just the wrong setting—"

"You idiot, listen to me. Actually listen to me. Think about what I'm telling you."

Officer Appleby says he has good news and bad news. He's in a better mood than he has been in weeks. He bounces across the living room, twirling a lanyard around his finger.

"The good news," Officer Appleby says, "is that you look healthy. Your ankle looks good. Is your ankle good?"

I tell him it's fine. Nice Appleby makes me a little sick.

"Good." He swings the lanyard so hard it wraps around his wrist. "Now for the bad news. You have that game at JamLand in a few days, correct?"

"Yea."

"You're going to lose that game." His hands go up. "I understand you're surprised." He plunges an imaginary knife into his heart. "*Et tu, Brutus?* I know. But I need you to you lose that game."

For a second, I'm a little dizzy. "You want us to lose?"

"Let me finish, Frank. Let me finish. As nice as your team is—and you've done some very nice, heartwarming things this summer—what are you really going to do in that league? We're talking real money here. Don't you think it'd be better used in the hands of someone else? Kids with real futures?"

I don't understand. "Kids with real futures?"

"This isn't personal, Frank. So here's another question: Did you know the chief's son plays for your opponent? He's a good kid, A student. Started a podcast on shark attacks or something. Ask yourself: Whose team would benefit more from this league? Your team, or a team full of A students with their own podcasts? Wouldn't it be a little wasteful to throw sponsorships away on a bunch of kids who might be locked up in a few months?"

Officer Appleby's voice bounces around my head, echoing until the words are all jumbled and I can't make sense of any of it. All I know for sure is that there's a thick heat filling my chest, rising into my face. "I don't really give a shit about the chief's son."

Officer Appleby drops his voice and puts a friendly hand on my shoulder. "Easy, easy, Frank. Last question: How many hours of community service have you done this summer?"

"Community service? You said playing basketball was good enough. You said that."

"Well, I guess I misspoke. I apologize for that. But as a Community Mentor and officer of the law, I have a responsibility to report anyone noncompliant with the terms of their probation to the local authorities. I should let you know that."

Then he pats me on the back and does a kind of two-step off the porch.

Back inside Mamá and Papá are dozing under a blanket and Tomás is jumping on the cushions, giggling every time someone on TV cusses. They look perfect, just the three of them. For a long time I just stand in the dark, watching. *Where's my Frankie?* I picture Mamá saying. *Where's my boy?* I imagine Papá saying. *Oh guys,* I'll laugh as I step out of the shadows, *you looking for me? I've been here the whole time!* And then they'd wave me over to the couch and let me pick something to watch. Is that so much to ask? But now they're all snoring softly, their chests rising and falling at the same time. No one's worried about ol' Frankie! No one cares!

As I walk to my room I start getting this feeling. It's like everybody everywhere is happy and smiling and has everything they want and then you look at your own life and it's crap. Might as well stop trying and just enjoy the crap because it's yours and what else you got? That was the best part of stealing that car: listening to the officers laugh at how ballsy I was on the way to the station.

Anyway, there's my Louisville Slugger under the bed. It's Little League–sized, from back when Papá wanted me to play, so you don't have to work that hard to get a good swing. You can crush a mailbox if you use your legs. It's got dents from trees, fire hydrants, telephone poles, Dumpsters, rearview mirrors. The handle feels good and cold. I tee up one of Tomás's Hulk action figures and knock it into the closet. Neon green splatters everywhere. Good to know I still got it. Here's my plan: take the bat on a walk. Walk until I find something that looks like it needs a good hit. Then hit it. Simple. Life is better when things are simple. Maybe I'll get in trouble and maybe I won't. What difference does it make?

Someone rings the doorbell and I'm sure it's Officer Appleby with more good news. I balance the bat on my shoulder and walk to the front door, taking deep, nervous breaths. I only open the door a crack. It's

Toni, standing in a little puddle of yellow light, snorting with laughter.

"Who did you think it was?" she asks. "The cops?"

I keep the door open a little. I almost wish it was Appleby. At least with him I know where I stand. But it's been three days since I tried to kiss Toni and looking at her now makes me want to bury my head somewhere.

"No," I say, "didn't know who it was."

She's wearing this white headband covered in purple and black swirls she's drawn on. "Ready for practice or what?"

"I'm not going today." But something in me goes soft and for a second I have this stupid vision of us practicing bounce passes together.

"You got something better to do?"

"Not feeling too good."

"Yeah, right," she says. She grabs my hand and pulls. I don't go right away, but I don't resist for too long, either. Before I'm all the way out I drop the bat behind the door. As we walk to the park, I'm scared she heard it ping against the floor, but she doesn't mention it. She's all smiles, jumping over cracks, telling me how much I'm going to love her painting.

"It's you, but if someone was looking through a kaleidoscope first," she says.

Somehow I feel worse. Why doesn't she hate me? It'd be better if she hated me. You mess up something good and people are supposed to hate you. That's how it works.

"The other day," I say. "Sometimes I do dumb things."

"It's cool," she says. She's walking too close to me, close enough that I can see the beads of sweat forming on her cheeks.

"No. You don't have to be nice. You can hate me if you want."

"Hate you? We're good, Frank. I'm happy we're friends. And I don't just leave my friends for no reason."

I slow down so that we can walk stride for stride. She asks me what's going on with my story, but I can't tell her that there's no more Jank and Moni. Jank was unfortunately hit by an asteroid and Moni was abducted and displayed at an intergalactic zoo. I crossed out the whole story one night, put a giant X over every word.

"Um," I say, "still figuring some things out. You got any ideas?"

"It's your story. You figure it out."

We get to the park just in time for warm-up stretching. I can't look nobody in the eye. Everyone's talking about the secret signs they'll use for their friends once we're on TV but I don't say anything. It's like I'm stuck in one of those dreams where you know it's a dream but you still can't wake up. The ball weighs a thousand pounds. Every time I mess up I apologize guiltily and run to punish myself before Coach Wise can. I didn't mean to miss that last lay-up—or did I? I don't know what's going on in my own head anymore. If I do the right thing and try to play I might get locked up. And if I do the wrong thing and try to lose I'll stay free. The guy who isn't supposed to hate me actually does, and the girl who's supposed to hate me doesn't. Left is right, forward is backward.

"You look kinda sick," Justin says after practice. "You good?"

"Yeah," I say. I try to smile. When we huddled at the end of practice, I felt his hand squeezing my shoulder. I thought he was playing but now it feels like a kind of message.

"Yeah, I'm good."

"I'm nervous, too." His hand comes back. "But don't even trip about tomorrow. It's gonna be dope. You always come through."

## Journal #6

Dear Officer Appleby,

    I figured I'd write directly to
you if you're going to be reading this
anyway. If you've read this far, you
know what three weeks of writing in
a journal gets you. Did it work? If
I'm back in junior court, I guess it
didn't. If I'm being all the way honest,
I'm not even sure what I learned.
    Maybe I should've been smarter
and just worried about myself today.
But where I'm from, that's not what
we do. I'm not trying to be no hero,
Officer Appleby. If it was anybody
else, I'd probably just do my own
thing, look the other way, and not
even worry about it. Truth be told
I've done that before. You probably
thought I was going to do that
today. When we walked in I saw how
you looked at us, almost like you
knew we were going to lose. You were

so confident! But the look on your face as the clock counted down! And the look on your face when Janae hit her fifth jumper in a row, when I threaded that pass to Justin! I wish I could've took a picture.

I know what you're thinking: All of this is really sweet, but what does it matter if you're locked up and can't even play? I don't really have an answer for you. But what would it mean to be free if I knew I betrayed everyone I really cared about? I mean, what kind of freedom is that?

Can I ask you a question, Officer Appleby? How'd it feel to throw me under the bus like you did? I thought we were cool. And here's another question: Are those officers really your friends? Guys who make fun of you and never come to your Bleeding Heart shows and force you to do crappy stuff to people you actually like? You call those friends?

Let me tell you about real friends. Real friends will look out for you so that you don't get blindsided by a screen. Real friends apologize when they're wrong and don't gloat when they're right. Real friends let you be exactly who you are, even if it's different from who they are. Where your real friends at, Officer Appleby?

Officer Appleby, I'm not saying I'm perfect. God knows I ain't perfect. I've cheated and stole before, but you already knew that. I almost lost a good friend the other day. If you look in this journal you'll see dumb stories I wrote for her. She's probably one of the best friends I ever had and I almost messed it up. But she didn't give up on me, which is the most amazing feeling you can ever have.

So I forgive you, Officer Appleby. I still think you're a nice guy.

I wasn't sure for a little while, but I really do think you're a good dude. I'm not giving up on you. As I've learned, sometimes nice guys get caught in bad situations and just try to make the best of it. So you had to make the best of your situation and I had to make the best of mine.

I don't regret it, Officer Appleby. I know I did the right thing.

Sincerely,

Frank Torres

**LJ Alonge** has played pickup basketball in Oakland, Los Angeles, New York, Kenya, South Africa, and Australia. Basketball's always helped him learn about his community, settle conflicts, and make friends from all walks of life. He's never intimidated by the guy wearing a headband and arm sleeve; those guys usually aren't very good. As a kid, he dreamed of dunking from the free-throw line. Now, his favorite thing to do is make bank shots. Don't forget to call "bank!"